¡FIESTA!

By **Ginger Foglesong Guy**
Pictures by **René King Moreno**

Greenwillow Books New York

Pastels, watercolors, and colored pencils
were used to create the full-color artwork.
The text type is Kabel Ultra Bold.

Printed in Hong Kong by South China Printing
Company (1988) Ltd.
First Edition   10   9   8   7   6   5   4   3   2   1

Library of Congress Cataloging-in-Publication Data

Guy, Ginger Foglesong.
¡Fiesta! / by Ginger Foglesong Guy ;
pictures by René King Moreno.
      p.   cm.
English and Spanish.
Summary: Bilingual text describes
a children's party and provides
practice counting in English and
Spanish.
ISBN 0-688-14331-8
[1. Parties—Fiction.   2. Counting.
3. Spanish language materials—Bilingual.]
I. Moreno, René King, ill.   II. Title.
PZ73.G84   1996   [E]—dc20
95-35848   CIP   AC

For my mother and father, who gave me Mexico,
and my brother and sisters, who shared it with me
—G. F. G.

For Zakkary, Spencer, and Anna
—R. K. M.

Una canasta
One basket

Dos trompetas
Two horns

¿Qué más?
What else?

Tres animalitos
Three little animals

¿Qué más?
What else?

Cuatro aviones
Four airplanes

¿Qué más?
What else?

Cinco trompos
Five tops

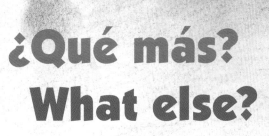

¿Qué más?
What else?

Seis chicles
Six pieces of gum

¿Qué más? **What else?**

Siete silbatos
Seven whistles

¿Qué más?
What else?

Ocho anillos
Eight rings

¿Qué más?
What else?

Nueve dulces
Nine candies

¿Qué más?
What else?

Diez serpentinas

Ten streamers

¡Niños!

Children!